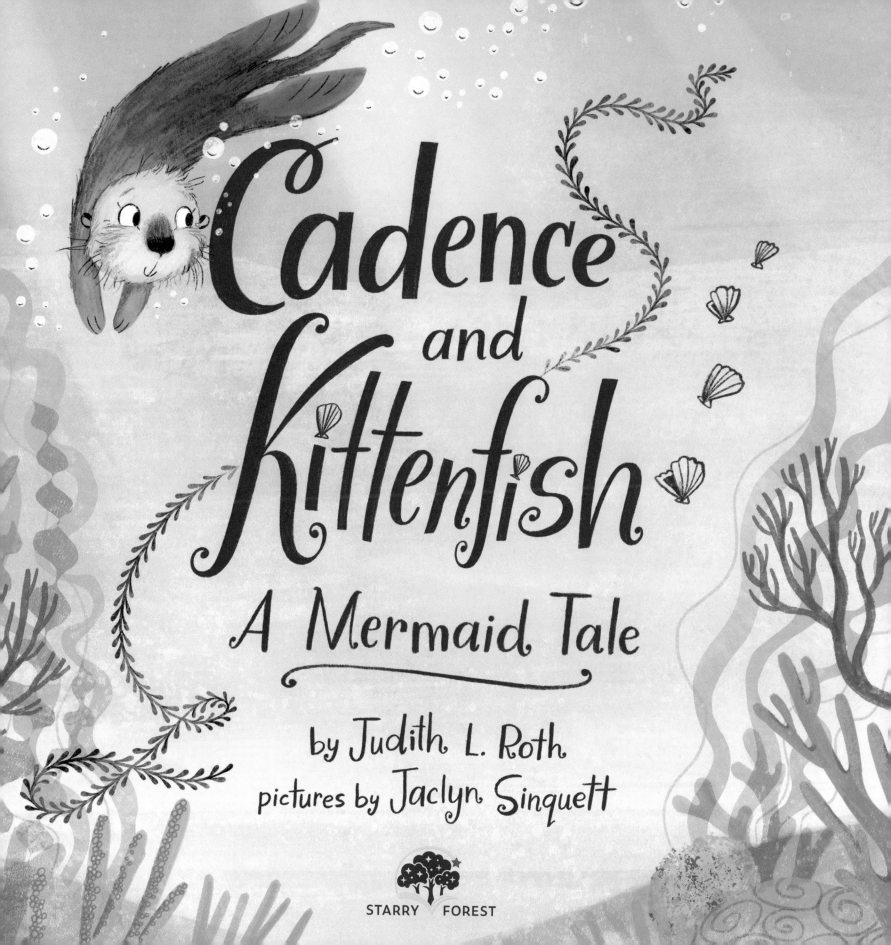

Cadence and Kittenfish

A Mermaid Tale

by Judith L. Roth

pictures by Jaclyn Sinquett

STARRY FOREST

Starry Forest® is a registered trademark of Starry Forest Books, Inc.
This 2022 edition published by Starry Forest Books, Inc.

First edition 2022

Library of Congress Catalog Card Number 2022933020
ISBN 978-1-951784-11-9 (picture book)
ISBN 978-1-951784-88-1 (ebook)
Manufactured in China
Lot #: 2 4 6 8 10 9 7 5 3 1
05/22

Starry Forest Books, Inc.
P.O. Box 1797
217 East 70th Street
New York, NY 10021

starryforestbooks.com | @starryforestbks

For five feisty young females I adore—
Riley, Taylor, Laura, Amber, and Lynnea.
—J. L. R.

For my first and very best friend, my mom.
—J. S.

*S*ince my mersisters swoosh away every morning
and leave me alone,
my days go like this:

... dance class with the dolphins.

Ding-dong-dashing
the fishermen.

Tai Chi with the
lighthouse keeper.

But . . . something is missing.

Kittens!

How did I not know about kittens?!

They're boomeranging on the rocks—

like a hurricane and a hug, all in one.

I *need* one!

I swim home and ask Dad for a kitten.

Dad says, "A catfish will have to do."

I say, "Eww. I want something adorable, not horrible."

Dad says, "Now Cadence, you've got a fishy tail
and you're adorable."
"Crabcakes!" I say.
I still want a kitten.

I zoom back to the frolicking fluffballs.

So sweet!

"Do you want to play, little hurricane?"

Hey! I got one!

Look how she leans into my scritches and kisses my nose.

Purrrr Purrrr

Adorable.

Now, where can we play together?

Underwater like the scuba divers!

With a bubble helmet so she can breathe.

We need to do something
about those claws.

Let's wrap them with seaweed
and make fantastic feline flippers!

Ready, Kitty?

Whoops!
This is not working.

Maybe a mermaid in a boat is better?

"Hey!" I say.

"That's my tail, not a tuna!"

Kittens are pointy in all
the wrong places.

How 'bout a floatie to keep kitty high and dry?

Ready, steady . . .

Oh dear.

I forgot about waves.

Kittens do not like water.

Not one little drip.

My hopes are dashed.

My kitten dreams have crashed.

Isn't there someone out there for me?
Someone comical and cute-iful
who can swim?
Someone not-a-cat.

Oh—someone just like that!

Look how he leans into my scritches
and kisses my nose.

Adorable.

Where have you been all my life,
you little kittenfish?